# MY BODY & ME

## KIM HARRIS

Illustrated by Navi' Robins

HG Publishing My Body and Me
2019 by Kim Harris
Published by HG Publishing Flint, Michigan Since 2019
ISBN: 978-1-7344865-0-6
Library of Congress Control Number: 2020900946
Illustrated by Navi' Robins

Hi, I'm Clair, I like dressing up and putting ribbons in my hair but playing with my friends in the park, now that's my favorite part.

And my name is Blair. Climbing trees in the park is my favorite place to be. Playing my guitar for all the people to see.

We are the twin panda bears. We like to share and help you be aware of where to go and what to do if bad people want to hurt you.

You've got your hands, you've got your feet,
and you've got your toes.

You've got your ears, you've got your mouth,
and you've got your nose.

You've got your eyes, you've got your heart,
but what about your other parts?

Blair, do you know your private parts are special?

My private parts are special, and just for me and no one else. Unless someone is helping me, I keep them to myself.

Do you know that your body is yours and no one has the right to touch your private parts?

No one can touch my private parts no matter who they are. Not my mother, not my father, or a friend near or far.

What if someone tries to touch your underwear?

You cannot touch my underwear. You cannot touch me down there. You cannot touch my underwear. You cannot touch me anywhere.

But what if someone tells you to keep a secret? I cannot, will not keep a secret. My mom and dad said don't keep it. You cannot touch my underwear.

You cannot touch me anywhere.

What if someone says you cannot tell because no one will believe you?

Mom and dad said I can tell them anything. Good or bad, happy or sad, they will listen to me.

You cannot touch my underwear. You cannot touch me anywhere. I cannot, will not keep a secret. My mom and dad said don't keep it.

What if someone wants to take pictures of your private body parts?

My private body parts are private because it's not for everyone to see.

You cannot see my private parts and cannot take pictures of me. You cannot touch my underwear.

You cannot touch me anywhere. I cannot, will not keep a secret. My mom and dad said don't keep it.

But what if your too scared to say no?

Even though I'm little I can use my voice. No one has the right to touch me, so I say NO. You cannot touch my underwear. You cannot touch me anywhere. I cannot, will not keep a secret, my mom and dad said don't keep it.

Who else can you tell if someone tries to hurt you?

If mommy and daddy ever forget, then I'll pull out my special list. A list of people who really care. People like you Panda Bear.

Now it's time for us to go. Time to let another child know how important they are. Remember to always use your voice.